Billionaire Seeks An Heir: Unraveled Lives

Misha Carver

This book is dedicated to my children who believed in me through the ups and downs of the writing process. My oldest son Brandon who told me to never take no for an answer, my second oldest, Daulton who taught me to fight for what I believe in, my youngest son Daniel who picked up after me tirelessly when my muse was keeping my fingers on the keyboard, and my daughter, Sarah who put up with listening to me go on and on about my stories.

Acknowledgments

It takes a village to raise a child and it takes a team to complete a book. I'd like to thank my editor, Claudette Cruz for putting up with my incredible misuse of commas.

I'd also like to thank my cover designer, Jacqueline Sweet. No matter how vague the information I give her, she always comes up with amazing designs on the fly.

More than anything, I'd like to thank you, the person reading this book. If not for you, this would only be paper with words written on it. Thank you so much for taking the time to read my stories. God bless.

Table of Contents

Chapter 1 ~ Jason

"IT'S NOTHING BAD I promise," I said as I took her hand in mine.

"Okay, Jason. What is it?" She bit her lip and looked down at the carpet.

"I don't really live here." I stared her in the eyes, waiting for her reaction.

"No kidding," she laughed. "Look, you don't need to feel embarrassed about where you live with me. I really care about you. Whose apartment is this anyway?"

"Oh, it's my apartment."

"I thought you said you didn't live here?"

"I don't. It's a long story Jerrica, but I'm not embarrassed about where I live. The truth is, I live in a big house, a very big house. I know I should have told you before, but I earn more in a week than most people earn in a year, or even two years. The trouble is that when you have that much money, it's hard to find someone who loves you for you and not what you can get them. When you told me you wanted to see my place, I freaked out a bit so I had my secretary rent and furnish this apartment for me."

"I see," she said as she got up and started walking toward the door.

"Wait, why are you leaving?" I got up and grabbed her by the elbow.

"What does that say about me, Jason? We've been dating for weeks now. You didn't want me to see your house because you didn't want me to know you had money. Why, because you were afraid I might want something from you? Guess what, sweetheart, I don't want a damn thing."

She tried to break my grip, but I wouldn't let her. "It's not like that, Jerrica. I have to be careful, really careful."

"You lied to me. Early on before you get to know someone I can see it. But after all the time we've spent together, no way. I thought I knew you, I mean really knew you. Tonight I found out that I don't know you at all. Now, if you'd get out of my way, I'd like to go home."

"I'm so sorry," I said as I reached for her other arm to pull her closer. "I didn't mean to lie to you, and maybe I did carry on the charade for a bit too long. The truth is that I only did it because I really care about you. I was afraid if you knew, something bad would happen and this would end, and I couldn't stand for that to happen."

"Would you please let go of me?" She was trying to pull away from me.

"No," I said as I pulled her even closer. "I even fake cooked dinner for you dammit. Now kiss me woman."

She burst into laughter. "How do you fake cook dinner?"

There was that beautiful smile that I loved. "I ordered takeout and put it in a pan."

"And yet, you still managed to burn it. I think you deserve a reward or something."

"I think so too," I said as I leaned over and kissed her soft lips. I finally let go of her arms so I could wrap mine around her. When I knew it was safe, I let go of her for a second. "Would you like to see my real house now?" I asked.

"Well, I don't know. I'm kind of hungry and some jerk just burned my dinner. I think I'm going to go see if some chump will take me to Burger King."

"Shut up and kiss me," I said as I pulled her close again. "I'll get Loretta to cook us something when we get there."

"Loretta?"

"She's my maid."

"Of course she is," she said as she grabbed her purse.

Chapter 2 ~ Jerrica

WHAT A JERK, I thought when he told me that he'd lied to me for weeks because he was afraid that I'd use him. I'd worked hard for everything I had, and I wasn't about to become dependent on any man.

I was determined to end it right then and there, to walk out on him. But the way he held my arms and controlled me, forced me to stay, and the look in his eyes when he apologized—he melted my heart all over again.

I was a little bit afraid to go to his house, especially after he mentioned the maid. But after I'd made such a big deal about him lying, I thought I'd better say yes. When we pulled up out front I almost peed my pants.

When he said a big house, he wasn't kidding. He lived in a damn mansion with pillars and a fountain out front, and a four-car garage to the side. I stood there for a few minutes just staring at the mammoth house in front of me.

"Hey, I told you it was big," he said.

I nodded. "That you did." We walked inside and he asked Loretta to cook us up some steaks. After we ate, we sat at the table and talked for a long time.

"So, do you still care about me?" he asked, giving me his cutest little boy look.

"Yes, just no more secrets," I said as I looked into his eyes intensely.

"No more secrets," he promised.

"So, when do I get to go on the grand tour of this house?" I asked. "I figure you must know this one a lot better than that apartment."

"Well, you know, Miss Rollins, there's no time like the present. Why don't you get up and I'll show you around?"

Chapter 3 ~ Jason

SHE GOT UP JUST as Rufus was coming in from his evening run. He came barreling in the door, pushed past Loretta, and jumped right up on her with his big muddy paws.

"Oh my God, I'm so sorry," I said as I put my arm around her to hold her steady. "Look at your dress. It's all covered in mud."

"That's okay," she laughed. "It'll wash. What the heck is this?"

"This here is my best friend in the whole world," I said as I scratched his ears and rubbed his back.

"He's adorable." She knelt down on the floor beside us and started rubbing his belly. "What kind of dog is he?"

"Well, when I got him, they told me he was a Great Dane, but as he got older he didn't look like any other Danes I'd seen. I did some investigating and found out that he also has Australian Shepherd and New-foundland in him."

"He's so cute," she said as she rubbed his ears. "What's his name?"

"Marmaduke," I said, trying hard not to laugh.

"Creative." She stared at me snidely with her eyebrow raised.

"No, I'm just teasing you. I've had old Rufus here since I first bought this house six years ago."

After we wrestled around with Rufus, she looked at the clock, and I knew she wanted to go home. I had hoped she'd decide to spend the night, but I didn't want to push my luck. She'd already forgiven me, and that was more than I could ask for.

I was glad that my secrets were finally out the open and that she knew who I really was. It was hard for me to take her to my real house because I was worried that at that point, it would all become about how much money I had. I should've known better with a girl like her.

Now that everything was in perspective, I could relax and let my guard down with her. I knew in my heart that everything would be smooth sailing from there on in. I finally found someone that I could share my life with, and everything that I'd worked so hard for.

Chapter 4 ~ Jason

ON MONDAY MORNING AS soon as I closed the door to my office and sat down behind my desk, Julie started knocking incessantly. At first I played with her and pretended I didn't hear the knocking. But then I decided that it wasn't fair to keep her in the dark after everything she'd gone through to help me.

"Come in," I said, pretending I didn't know who was there. She came waltzing in acting nonchalant.

"Can I help you with something?" I asked her as I looked up at her, trying to remain expressionless.

"Well?" she said, with her hands in the air like she was expecting me to tell her something. I knew damn well she was expecting me to tell her something. Of course she wanted to know how things went. I just wanted to see how long it would take her to come right out and say it.

"Well, what? Is there something I can help you with?" I was enjoying humoring her and watching her get impatient with my antics.

"Jason, you know full well what I want to know. How did things go on Friday night? Did Miss Rollins like the apartment?"

"Ha ha, well she loved the apartment and my grand tour, which may I tell you went over like a lead balloon. It would have helped if I had gone in to check it out first."

"What you mean?" She folded her arms and stared at me. "You didn't even check out the apartment until that night? What, are you crazy?"

"Well, I mean, it was just an apartment. I didn't think it would be that difficult. It's a few rooms in a small box. How hard can it be to give somebody a tour?" I said as I looked at her shyly, realizing what a huge mistake I'd made.

"I knew I should have gone over there with you a few days beforehand to help you sort it all out. I know you and I know how you procrastinate. I should have known that you would just leave this to the last second and everything would fall apart at the seams. So how big of a mess you make?"

"Fortunately, Miss Rollins is very forgiving. It really wasn't that bad at all. I mean, other than telling her that I piss in my linen closet, dream about her while I'm sitting on the toilet, and setting the kitchen on fire, everything went fine. It really wasn't that bad at all."

"You have got to be kidding. You didn't even look around the apartment when you got there?"

"Julie, I didn't have time. I had to put the dinner on the stove so it would be ready when she got there."

"Well, at least you cooked for her. That's a good start anyway," she said as she shook her head.

"I wouldn't exactly call it cooking," I said as I smiled and tapped my pen on the desk.

"Oh God, what did you do now?" She tapped her foot on the floor and glared at me, waiting for an answer.

"Nothing bad. I just couldn't cook. I tried a bunch of recipes and burned every one of them. Nothing was working out right, so I bought some takeout, I threw it in some pans and I put it on the stove. Simple, right? Easy peasy."

"Let me guess, that's how you started the fire?"

"You got it, sweetheart."

"And after all that she's still dating you?" she asked with a gleam in her eye and a smile on her face.

"At that point I decided it was time to tell her the truth. I sat her down and explained to her that it wasn't my apartment. Then I took her to my house and introduced her to Rufus."

"And she was okay with all that secret-keeping?" she asked as she stared at me intensely.

"At first she was mad, but then I explained everything to her and she understood my reasons. Of course, I had to promise that I wouldn't keep any more secrets from her."

"Well, that's better then. At least she knows that you own the company now and everything and get back to normal."

"I didn't exactly get to that part. I took her to my house and I told her I had money. But I didn't tell her that I own Donnelly Multimedia. Speaking of which, I need another favor from you."

"You promised her no more secrets and you still haven't told her that you're her boss? When are you going to learn? If this whole thing falls apart, you're going to have nobody but yourself to blame."

"I just really don't think it's time to tell her that not only am I her boyfriend, but I'm also her boss."

"Okay, but I'm not responsible for whatever happens. What do you need this time?"

"I was thinking it would be nice if she had a few more job responsibilities. She wishes her job was more exciting, and she's worked hard for this. I'd like to move her on up the ladder bit."

"Oh, Jason, this whole thing is going to backfire in your face. When she finds out, and she will find out, she is going to lose it. You can't just go around promoting her every time you feel like it. She's going to feel like she didn't get any of these promotions on her own merit."

"But Julie, she deserves them. She really does. She's a hard worker and a fast learner. I've been tracking her accomplishments and performance here at Donnelly Multimedia and she is a real go-getter. If HR had been keeping a closer watch she would've gotten these promotions without my help."

"That might be how you see it, but all she's going to see is that she slept with the boss and rose to the top. What do you think that's going to do to her self-esteem?"

"Look, this is the last time. I promise I won't ask again. The next promotion will be on her own merit."

"Okay, where do you want me to put her now? Last time I moved her into an associate PR role in new series development. That's a pretty demanding job, and she's been doing excellent over there. I'm worried that if you move around too much it might get confusing, and you might be setting her up to fail."

"I know," I said as I rested my elbows on my desk and folded my hands in front of me. "I'm thinking instead of associate PR we step her up to senior PR or head of PR in that division."

"Oh, you can't do that. Seriously, people will be pissed. Do you know how many people have been trying to get that position?" she said as she waved her hands around in the air.

"She's worked hard for it. She deserves it." I stretched my arms out across my desk and stared her down.

"And they don't?" she asked accusingly. "Many of those people have been here a lot longer than she has."

"They have, but I've checked out their files to and I haven't seen the same dedication and drive from the other employees. I'm not looking at this lightly, Julie. I've put a lot of thought into it, but I don't think it would be fair to give the position to anyone else."

"Hey, there's nothing I can say. You're the boss. Consider it done. I'm just glad it's your funeral and not mine." She turned and walked out of my office shaking her head. I could tell she was becoming more and more frustrated with the game I was playing.

Chapter 5 ~ Jerrica

WHEN I GOT HOME from Jason's house that night Liz was waiting for me, excited to hear about my dinner at his place.

"What was it like? Was he a good cook?" she asked the second I walked through the door.

"Oh my God, Liz, I had an amazing time. Turns out he just doesn't have a little tiny apartment. He lives in this huge house with water fountains out front and pillars and a huge dog named Rufus."

"You've got to be kidding, tell me more."

"No, no, I'm serious. I couldn't believe it. The guy is freaking loaded, man. I'm still in shock."

"It's like you hit the jackpot, sweetheart," Liz said she munched away on her potato chips and sipped her wine.

"How are things going with you and Jimmy?" I asked her as I poured myself a glass of wine.

"Things are going okay. We're going to see each other again this weekend. He's still pretty hung up on his ex-wife, though. I don't know. It's all he talks about, and I don't want to spend all of my time competing with her memory."

"Yeah, I suppose that can be a little rough. I wouldn't like that either. Know what's funny? I don't even know if Jason has an ex-girlfriend. Well, obviously he does, but he's never mentioned any of them."

"Well then, consider yourself a very lucky girl. At least you won't have the haunting memory of the ex to deal with. One thing's for sure, he's not the jerk we thought he was the night we first met him, or at least he doesn't appear to be."

"Well, I wouldn't count anything out yet, you just never know. I'm still playing it careful."

"Yeah, I don't blame you. I wouldn't want to get into anything too quickly either. You just never know these days. So how are things going at work?"

"Still the same old, same old. It's not quite as exciting as I'd like, but it is a lot of fun to see how new series are developed and work with the actors and stuff. How are things going for you?"

"Things are going okay. I've given some thought to moving back home with the 'rents. I had a good time there a couple weeks ago and I might just go back there for a while, you know, to see how things go. I won't leave you screwed, though. I'll wait until you find a new roommate."

"Hey, don't worry about me. If you need to go back home, it's okay. I understand completely. No worries."

"Yeah, but I don't want to leave you stuck here. I'll hang around until you can find someone to take my spot."

"That's no biggie. What's putting an ad in the paper? Somebody else will pick it up within a couple weeks. You know that. If it will help you figure things out with Jimmy you go ahead."

"You know what would be easier? Why don't you just move in with Jason?" She looked at me with that mischievous grin on her face, waiting to see my reaction.

"No, no, no. It's way too soon to be even thinking that far ahead." I sat down on the couch and put my feet up on the coffee table. I couldn't imagine myself living with any man, at least not yet.

"Oh, that's what you have in mind. I can tell either you want to have him move in here or you want to live there. Considering that he has a bigger house, and the big dog, that's where I'd go."

"Well, you never know what could happen down the road, but I don't think that's going to happen right away. I think that for now I'll probably either get another room-mate or stick it out here on my own for a little while and see how things go. What do you say we catch a movie?"

"Jerrica, it's like one o'clock in the morning and we both have to work tomorrow. Do you seriously want to go to the movies?"

"No," I said as I tossed the throw pillow at her. "I meant on the television."

"Oh yeah, sure. Why don't you take a look through and see if there's anything good on, while I grab us each another glass of wine?"

"Yes, that sounds good. Want to grab another bag of chips out of the cupboard while you're at it?"

ON MONDAY MORNING WHEN I went to work the day started like any other. I had to go through the spreadsheets, check on what series were in development, talk to the screenwriters, talk to the actors, and arrange for interviews. Everything was going according to plan.

Then Michael Plotkin, the actor on a new series called *The Educators,* decided to drop a monkey wrench in my entire day. Set in his drama queen ways, he decided to throw a fit that he couldn't attend the Esquire interview because he was going to be too busy getting his hair done. I hated having to run interference with primadonnas.

"Michael, what the hell are you doing?" I asked him. "You know how important this interview is to the series launch."

"Jerrica, I'm not going. That's when my hair appointment is. I will go for the interview afterwards or another day," he said as he waved his index finger in my face.

"No no no, that is when the interview was booked for, and you're going." I wanted to grab that finger of his and snap it right off.

"I told you I am not going then. I have plans and that time is not a good time for me." He folded his arms in front of himself and pouted.

"Look," I said as I stared him in the eyes. "If this series doesn't debut in the top ten you could be canceled in the first six weeks, so I suggest you change your hair appointment and you make it to that interview." I raised my eyebrow at him and tapped my foot.

He was really starting to piss me off. My job was at stake, and I wasn't about to play games over his curly locks.

"Well, what if I drop out of the series? Then there is no series and then the network goes down. What would Donnelly Multimedia do without me? What do you have to say about that?" I could not believe what I was hearing.

"Are you serious? Do you have any idea how replaceable you are? Don't start playing games here, Mister, because you will be out the door. Now, I'd suggest you get yourself ready to change your hair appointment. You make plans to get down to that interview, and that's final."

I stormed out of his dressing room and back to my office. I could not believe how difficult actors were to work with. I sat down at my desk and started going through the paperwork again, trying to figure everything out.

As I planned for the week ahead, I knew there would be more obstacles thrown my way because that's just the way it went when you dealt with people who felt like the world owed them everything.

When lunchtime finally rolled around, I was thrilled. I had already made plans to meet up with Jason at the Astor Café on the corner of fifty-seventh and third. I was really looking forward to seeing him. I knew that just spending some time with him would ease my nerves and calm my spirit.

As soon as I saw the clock roll around to noon, I couldn't get out of that office fast enough. I grabbed my purse, rushed out the doors, and scurried along the sidewalk until I made it in the doors of the Astor.

When I got there, the host asked me if I wanted a table for one. I said, "I believe there's a reservation for Jason Donnelly?"

"Yes," she said. "Right this way." I followed her through the busy restaurant to a small table off in the corner by a window with a beautiful view of the city. I glanced over the menu briefly as I sat there, barely able to contain myself while I waited for Jason's arrival.

Finally, I heard the familiar sound of his voice as he approached the table. I stood up to greet him as he took me in his arms and hugged me tight.

"It's wonderful to see you, Jerrica," he said as he kissed me.

"So great to see you too, Jason. I had a wonderful time the other night."

"I know, me too, and I'm so sorry about all the secrets of everything that happened."

"That's all behind us now that everything is out in the open and on the table. We don't have to worry about keeping secrets anymore."

"So how is your job going," he asked me as he glanced over the menu.

"It's going okay," I said as I set my water glass down on the table. "One thing I've learned is that actors can be a real pain. For some reason they think that they are better than everyone else, and that their hair appointment comes before an interview or even their entire series."

"Ha ha, I bet they do," he said as he gave me a knowing smile.

"How are things going for you and your work? You told me that you work in corporate finance or something like that?"

"Oh, seriously, so boring. You don't even want to hear about that. Your job is much more interesting than mine."

"I guess I might be taking on a second job soon," I said as I glanced out the window, watching the passersby.

"What do you mean?" he said as he reached out his hand to touch mine.

"Last night my roommate Liz told me that she is moving back home with her parents. I'm going to be screwed. I'm either going to have to move or find another roommate."

"Why don't you move in with me? I have plenty of room in my big old house. It's just me and Rufus and the maid, there's lots of room there for you."

"Jason, I really think it's way too soon for us to move in together. I don't even want to talk about that at this point."

"Listen, it would fix your problem, I'd be less lonely, and old Rufus would love it."

"Jason, I'm not Cinderella and I don't need to be rescued. I'm sorry, but if you're looking to be a hero then you're barking up the wrong tree. For right now, I'll solve my own problem. Maybe someday when the time is right, we'll move in together, but right now is not the time."

We sat and chatted through lunch while we laughed and shared stories. I was having so much fun that I almost lost track of time. By the time I glanced at my watch I had ten minutes to get back to the office.

"Oh God, Jason. I've got to get back. I'm so sorry, but I have one million things to do to get ready for the series launch and I'm going to be late."

"That's okay," he said as he stood up to hug me goodbye.

I headed back to the office and started trying to arrange more interviews to get ready for the big launch. After about an hour my supervisor called me into his office. *Goddamned Michael,* I thought. *He had to go whine about how I tried to stand my ground with him.* Now I was going to get in shit and would probably lose my job.

That was the last thing I needed when everything was going wrong. I put my palms out flat on my desk and stood up, taking a deep breath. The only thing I could do was firmly stand my ground once again to try to get through to these people that business was business.

As soon as I walked into his office and closed the door behind me, Mr. Mercury stared up at me from his desk.

"Jerrica," he said. I could feel my palms getting sweaty and my legs starting to shake, but I wasn't about to let him know that my confidence had been knocked down.

"Yes Mr. Mercury," I said, with my hand on my hip, waiting for whatever he was about to throw it me.

"I want to talk to you about your performance on the job in our department. I've been looking through your employee file and…"

"Look, if this is about Michael I just want to make it very clear that he needs to understand that interviews come before his goddamned hair. I don't care what else he's got going on, but this launch is way more important than whether or not he has a hair out of place."

"It's not about that, Jerrica. This is about your performance on the job. It has nothing to do with any one individual."

As soon as he said it, I started to question everything I had done since I'd been in my new position. Had I been screwing up the entire time? Had I been taking myself too seriously? Perhaps I hadn't been doing anything right.

"As I said, I've been looking through your file and I've discovered that you've been doing an exemplary job since you've been in this position. I'm prepared to offer you a senior PR position in series development with options for further advancement."

"Really? Are you serious?"

"As serious as I could ever be. You'll have your own office, and you won't have to deal directly with the actors anymore. Instead, you'll be dealing with the associate public relations people and assigning their duties. You won't have to worry about actors and their attitudes unless an associate is having an issue, and then you'll need to step in. Are you interested in the position?"

"Yes, of course. That would be wonderful."

"Great, your new office is right around the corner. Why don't you start moving your things today?"

"Okay, when do I start in my new role?"

"How does tomorrow morning sound?"

"Tomorrow morning sounds wonderful."

"Great. Now along with your new position come new duties. Your first assignment will be to make a presentation at the board meeting tomorrow morning."

"A presentation at the board meeting? How do I do that? I haven't even been to one of the board meetings. What is the presentation about?"

"Jerrica, if you're not sure how to do your job, maybe I should rethink this promotion," Mr. Mercury said as he folded his hands across his desk while he stared at me.

"No. I know I can do the job. You just have to tell me what it entails and what we need to do at this board meeting," I said.

"I'd like you to discuss new series launches in the last three years, what the points of success are, and what the points of failure are. I'd also like you to discuss how we can hit the ground running with each new series this season. While you're at it, make a point of mentioning where you think we are and are not hitting the mark with the series that we have lined up for the season."

"And I need to have this all ready for to-morrow morning?" I asked as I began think-ing about the season's lineup and started planning the layout of my presentation in my mind.

"I'm not going to lie to you. It's going to take some research on your part and you're going to be a very busy girl tonight. Tell me now. Can you do the job or not?"

"I can do it and I'll have it ready. Tomorrow morning I will wow you with the most amazing presentation that you have ever seen. Everyone in that boardroom will be blown away, I promise you that."

"I'll hold you to your words, Jerrica. Don't let me down."

Chapter 7 ~ Jerrica

AS SOON AS I got home from work Liz wanted to talk.

"Hey, how was work today?" she asked as she poured us both a glass of wine.

"Not bad. I got another promotion," I said. "But I'm afraid that I'm not able to drink too much of this stuff tonight. I've got to do a presentation at a board meeting tomorrow and I am going to be up to my eyeballs in work all night long to get this up to snuff."

"Presentation before the board? Wow, that's pretty serious. You must be excited."

"No, scared to death is more like it. I don't know what the hell I'm doing. I've never been to one of the board meetings before. I have no idea what it is that I'm supposed to do."

I took a sip of my wine and set the glass down and stared up at the ceiling, trying to make sense of the ideas that were running through my head.

"Did they give you any sense of direction whatsoever?" Liz asked.

"Yes. I'm supposed to explain the series that they've run the last three years and what made them work, what made some not work. They also want me to talk about the series that are coming out this season, which ones I think will make it and why, and where I think we're hitting the mark."

"It sounds to me like they gave you a pretty good roadmap," she said as she folded her arms in front of herself. "You're a smart girl. You just need to put some ideas together based on that you know you like and what you don't like on TV. You know what the ratings are and you know what's coming out during the season. You work directly with the actors and you should be able to put together a killer presentation in record time."

"That's easy for you to say, but you're not the one doing it," I said as I bit my lip and played with my pen.

"Well, you got me there. But I'm sure you'll do great. Anyway, I'm going out tonight with some friends so you can get some work done. You'll have the place all to yourself."

"Where are you going?"

"Nunnu."

"Nunnu?" I asked curiously.

"None of your business. I'm just going out. You stay here and get your work done. Have a wonderful night and do a killer presentation tomorrow, okay."

I sat there drinking back wineglass after wineglass, thinking about each series that were played on the network for the last three years. I contemplated what I liked about them and what I didn't as well as what the ratings were.

My mind wandered to what got canceled and what got renewed. I was almost ready to pull my hair out trying to figure out what the IT factor was, especially when it came to the new series and how I was supposed to know what we were hitting the mark with and what we weren't.

And then it hit me. The IT factor isn't the same every year. The IT factor changes year after year as the audience changes. People evolve and the audience evolves. One year a television show like Mr. Donovan from four years ago was a hit, where today it would be canceled after two episodes.

This year *The Educators* might be a hit, but five years from now it might be canceled after six showings. There is no way of knowing what's going to hit the ground running before the first episode hits the air. Even then you don't know until after maybe the first nine or ten episodes or even the first season has played out.

People don't always tune into the first episode. Sometimes they don't tune in until halfway through the season. Sometimes they don't until the second season, and that's why sometimes shows get picked up that maybe shouldn't. The unfortunate thing is that sometimes a network will cancel a series halfway through the first season when it hasn't even had a chance to gain an audience.

I started to put my presentation together based on that, hoping that I was on the right track and that I wasn't going to make a fool of myself at the meeting. I made up some index cards with my speech and I made a PowerPoint presentation slideshow explaining everything about the different shows and how everything evolves with audiences and television and the ratings. By the time I was done it was four o'clock in the morning and I was convinced that I had done a bang-up job.

I was almost tempted to just stay up, but I decided that it might be a good idea to get a little bit of sleep so that I was fresh for the presentation. I set my alarm for 7:00 a.m. and decided to crash on the couch for three hours. My telephone alarm woke me up instantly as soon as it went off.

I jumped in a quick shower, grabbed a cup of coffee, and ran out of the door ready to present my presentation. As soon as I got to Donnelly Multimedia I waltzed into my new office and sat down behind my new beautiful oak desk, running my fingers across the top of it.

My name plaque hadn't arrived yet. That's when I knew my position would be official, when I had the name plaque for my desk and the name plaque for my door. They were supposed to come that day, and I could hardly wait. I didn't expect they'd be there until after my presentation, though.

A knock at the door pulled me out of my daydream.

"Hello," I said.

Mr. Mercury turned the knob and poked his head in. "Is the presentation ready?" he asked with a grin on his face.

"I'm as ready as I'll ever be," I said. "Do you have facilities for a slideshow?" He looked at me and grinned. I knew he realized that I put a lot of thought and work into this presentation.

"Yes, we do. I'll get that all set up for you. The meeting is in thirty minutes in boardroom D. I'll see you there."

"Okay, sounds good. I'll be ready."

My pulse was racing. I was so nervous. I knew I was ready for this, but at the same time I couldn't believe that I was addressing the board of Donnelly Multimedia. I had to prove myself. I'd come so far in such a short period of time, and I wanted to keep climbing the ladder. The best way to do it was to show them what I was made of, and this presentation was the perfect opportunity.

As I got closer to the time to head down to the boardroom my stomach was getting queasy and I could feel myself getting more and more nervous. I kept taking deep breaths and trying to remain calm. Five minutes before I had to be there I grabbed my paperwork and my laptop and headed on down the hall towards boardroom D.

I could hear all the voices in the room and I started to panic. I gathered myself together outside the door and I walked in. Everyone greeted me as I made my way to the head of the table. Suddenly the door opened again.

I turned around to see Jason standing there in a suit. My jaw dropped to the floor and my knees went weak.

"Jerrica, have you met Jason Donnelly?" Mr. Mercury asked.

Suddenly it all made sense—Jason Donnelly, Donnelly Multimedia, all the promotions since I met him. My boyfriend was my boss. I wanted to crawl under a rock and stay there. I was embarrassed, upset and angry. I didn't know what to do. I closed my eyes for a brief second and then I extended my hand.

"I'm afraid we haven't been formally introduced," I said. "My name is Jerrica Rollins."

Jason looked at me funny and I could tell he knew that I was angry. He went along with it though, shook my hand and told me it was nice to meet me.

I was so nervous and so upset during the presentation that I dropped my paperwork, my index cards flew everywhere, and I fumbled through my slideshow. I was so furious with him for having lied to me. We had promised each other no more secrets, and he turned around and kept the biggest secret of all from me.

After I got through the meeting, I told Mr. Mercury that I was feeling ill and I went home for the rest of the day. I just could not deal with him and I needed to get out of there as fast as I could.

*J*ESUS CHRIST, WHY THE *hell did they have her do a presentation at the board meeting?* I should've known this was going to happen sooner or later, but you'd think they would clear that with me first. From the look on her face when I went walking in that room, I could tell that she never wanted to see me again.

I tried to go to her office afterwards, but they told me she had gone home sick. I called her cell and her landline multiple times, but she didn't answer. I even tried emailing her, to no avail. I couldn't stand the thought of losing her over something so stupid.

I sat behind my desk and tried to get some work done, but I couldn't get her off my mind. When I couldn't take it anymore, I got up and headed out the door.

"Julie," I said as I walked past her desk, "hold all my calls for the rest of the day. I have a very important meeting and I won't be back."

"But Jason, you have three important appointments this afternoon," she said as she followed behind me.

"Just tell them I'm sick," I said as I stormed out the door. I got in my car and headed towards Jerrica's place, trying to figure out what I would say to her when I got there. I hoped that she would forgive me for this one last lie. I knew it was a lot to ask. I could tell that her heart was shattered in the meeting. I had to make it up to her somehow.

No matter how hard I thought I could not come up with the perfect words. The only thing that made sense was "I'm sorry," and I hoped that it would be good enough. I stopped on the way and picked her up some green lilies which she had told me previously were her favorite flowers. I didn't know if they would be a good enough icebreaker, but a guy had to have hope.

I knocked on her door, praying she'd answer. When I heard footsteps, I was elated, thinking that she had decided to forgive me. I heard the door handle turn and waited in anticipation to see her beautiful face. When the door opened her roommate stood there glaring at me. I remembered that stare. It was the same as the one she'd given me that night at the bar.

"Hello," she said as she looked at me.

"Hi, I'm here to see Jerrica," I stammered, feeling like a schoolboy meeting the parents for the first time.

"She's not here right now," Liz replied.

"Do you know when she'll be in?" I asked, knowing full well that she was there.

"Look, I really don't think she wants to talk to you right now. She's pretty upset."

"Liz, that's your name, right? Liz, isn't it?"

"Yes."

"Can I talk to you for a second? Look, it's like this. I feel really, really bad. I didn't mean to keep that from her. I probably should've told her that night I took her to my house. But how do you tell someone that you're their boss after you've kept it a secret for so long?"

"Jason, how do you not tell her? I don't understand how you kept everything from her for so long and then the very night you promised her no more lies, you knew you were keeping an even bigger secret. I just don't understand what made you think this would be okay."

"I didn't really think it would be okay. I just didn't think that far ahead. I just wanted everything to work out perfectly between us and I thought if she knew certain things, it wouldn't."

"Well, now she knows certain things and knows that you kept them from her, and it's still not going to. I guess the truth was your undoing either way, by the looks of things."

"I really need your help here, Liz. I love her. I can't lose her over this. Please, can I just talk to her?"

"She's going to kill me, but come in," she said as she opened the door and stepped aside.

I walked in the apartment slowly, terrified that furniture was going to come hurtling across the room at me. At first I didn't see her and I wondered if maybe she wasn't actually there. Then I heard footsteps come walking down the hall and I saw her wavy blonde hair. When she looked up I saw her red, swollen eyes filled with tears and I knew that I had caused them.

In that instant I felt terrible. I never wanted to make her hurt like that again. I held out the green lilies, hoping that somehow they could heal her heart. She looked at me as if I'd lost my mind.

"Jason, do you really think this could fix everything that you've done? I went there to Donnelly Multimedia as a new college graduate, believing that I could take on the world. I worked hard at my job. I did everything I could to climb the ladder. Then I met you. Suddenly I get two wonderful promotions and raises, and I think it's because of the wonderful job that I'm doing. Little do I know it's because I'm dating the boss. Now I feel like the laughingstock of the entire place, and I was the last one to find out. How could you, Jason? How could you do that to me?"

"It wasn't like that. When I first met you, I didn't even know you worked for Donnelly Multimedia. I didn't know until that first day that we met for lunch. And even then I couldn't tell you because I was afraid you wouldn't want to date me. Even more so, I wanted you to love me for me and not for my money or what I could get you. I needed to know that I was important to you, and not my money. But you don't have to worry about being the laughingstock of anything. Nobody knows we're seeing each other. All these raises and promotions you've been getting are based on your employee file and nothing else. They're not based on who you're dating. It's just been a review of your file each and every time. What caused your file to be reviewed might have been me. But, if your file had not been stellar, you would've not gotten one of those promotions, I can guarantee you that."

"So you're telling me that dating you had nothing whatsoever to do with those promotions?"

"Yes, that's exactly what I'm telling you. If your employee record had sucked you'd still be a bottom feeder doing the gopher job that you were doing when you first started, sweetheart. Nobody has to promote you just because…"

"Just because the boss says so," she said as she glared at me through slanted eyes.

"Look, I really am sorry. I didn't need to go this far. I kept secrets from you for way too long. In the beginning, it was important to make sure that you weren't after my money. After a while I should've let you in. I didn't and this is all my fault. I'll take the blame for that. The night we said no more secrets, I should've told you about this. But I was afraid that you would turn around and walk out right then and there. I didn't want to take that risk. Now I'm going to turn around and go give you some time to think. I hope you come around and call me later tonight, but if you don't, I'll understand. I'd like you to take this time to think about what it's like to be in my position and how difficult dating can be for me. When you think about that, maybe, just maybe, you'll understand."

The hardest thing I ever did was turning around and walking out of her apartment. I was taking a chance and I knew it. My heart felt like it was going to beat out of my chest, knowing that there was a very real possibility that I'd never hear from her again.

I went back to the office, even though I told Julie I wouldn't be back because I knew that there was no way I could occupy myself at home enough to stop thinking about her. Somehow I managed to get through the rest of my workday before I went home.

To be truthful, the real reason I went back to the office was to wait and see if she called and quit, because I half expected her to. At home I wouldn't know about it until the next day. Fortunately, she didn't, so I felt a little bit more positive, but she still hadn't called me.

Chapter 9 ~ Jason

THE NEXT DAY WHEN I went into the office Julie stopped me at her desk. A feeling of terror came over me when I saw the look on her face. I thought for sure Jerrica had quit.

"What is it?" I asked as I looked down at the floor with my hands in my pockets.

"It's Jerrica. She said she's not feeling well today and she's running a few minutes late." I looked up at Julie and smiled.

"So she's actually coming in?" I asked her.

"Yes, and I think you should consider yourself very lucky. I don't know how you get away with some of the things you do, Jason. This girl must really love you. Don't screw it up."

I didn't run into Jerrica for the rest of the day. I made a point of not trying to. I knew that she probably needed some space, and we'd never run into each other at work before. I figured she'd call me after work if she wanted to.

The important thing to me was that she was still coming to work, and the lines of communication were still open. As I was getting into my car after work, I received a text message.

Want to talk?

It was from Jerrica. I was excited about the possibility of talking to her, but terrified that she was going to break up with me. I answered her anyway.

Yes. When?

I stared at my phone, waiting for her answer. It seemed like an eternity before I heard the ringtone again.

How about now?

I looked up from my phone and she was standing in front of me with a smile on her face. I was so relieved to see her.

"I am so sorry," I said. "I will spend the rest of my life making this up to you. I honestly never meant to hurt you. It was never my intention."

"I know," she said. "I get it. I just wish you felt like you could be more open with me. I think we need to make an agreement to be more honest and open with each other going forward. Before we said no more secrets, but there were still secrets. From now on, promise me that there are no more secrets."

"No, you're right. We shouldn't have any more secrets. This has totally backfired and I never meant for it to hurt you. It's clear that secrets will make or break our relationship, and I think we need to keep everything on the table from here on in."

"So what do you say we take Rufus for a walk in the park?" she said as she smiled at me with a gleam in her eye.

"I think Rufus would really enjoy that," I answered. "Your car or mine?"

I KNEW THE MINUTE he came to my house with the lilies that I was going to forgive him. It was only a matter of time. There was no way I could leave my job and there was no way I could ever leave him. After work the next day we got into his car and went to get Rufus to take him for a walk in the park.

I loved that big old guy. While we walked and held hands, we stopped by an ice cream stand and grabbed three cones.

One for me, one for Jason, and of course, one for Rufus.

Now that everything was on the table and there were no more secrets hiding in the shadows, I knew that everything was going to be perfect between us going forward.

"Hey, want to come back to the house and I'll cook you dinner for real this time," Jason said with a grin on his face.

"I'm not sure if that's a risk I'm willing to take," I laughed.

"I promise not to set the house on fire this time," he teased as he chased after Rufus.

"I'm not sure. Do you think you have enough insurance for that place?" I said sarcastically.

"I don't know, but I do have a few fire extinguishers."

"I hope you have some baking soda too," I laughed.

"Hey, you just stop," he teased. "How about I take you to dinner instead?"

"Or I could cook you dinner," I offered.

"You know what, after everything I've put you through how about tonight's on me. Anywhere you want to go, you name it."

"Why don't you surprise me?" I said as I smiled up at him.

He looked at me and I could tell a light bulb went off in his head. "I know the perfect place," he said. "Let's drop Rufus off and go."

We dropped Rufus off at his house and headed out. I had no idea where we were going, but it was okay as long as I was with him. As we drove down the winding streets of the busy city, I stared out the window and thought about how lucky I was. All of those people who were whizzing past us in their vehicles couldn't possibly know how happy I was in that moment.

When his car finally stopped I laughed when I realized we were parked in front of Sparky's bar and pool room, the very place where it all began. The place where I had first met him, just a few months ago.

"I thought we were going for dinner," I laughed.

"We are, but I thought we'd have a drink first. Shall we?" he said as he looked at me and grinned.

"I'm game if you are." I started to open my door, but he stopped me.

"No, you just wait there," he said. He came around and opened the door for me and we went into the bar for a drink. As we approach the bar, he asked the bartender for two glasses of white wine.

"I thought you were a beer drinker," I said as I grinned at him.

"I am, but tonight is cause for celebration."

"And what are we celebrating?" I asked.

"Tonight we're celebrating us. We're not just celebrating us, but we're celebrating a new paradigm of us. This is a new beginning where there are no secrets, where we have nothing to hide. From this day forward, we'll share everything with each other, and we're not going to keep our relationship a secret anymore either."

I took a sip of wine and I looked up at him. "Are you sure that's such a good idea?" I said.

"What? Isn't this what you want, no secrets, no hiding…"

"It might make things harder at work when people find out we're dating. It might be a better idea to keep it under wraps for a while longer."

"You can't have it both ways. You have to decide what you want. I'm ready for our relationship to be public, are you?"

"If you're sure this is what you want, then it's okay with me," I said. "I'm a little nervous about the office, but I'm sure we can work that out."

"Don't worry," he said as he put his hand on my shoulder. "Everything's going to be just fine now. There's nothing else to worry about."

"I know. I just can't help but wonder if something else is going to topple everything over."

"There is nothing else that could possibly destroy our relationship. We've dealt with at all."

After our drink we went out to the Galloping Buffalo for dinner. I'd never eaten there before and I had a great time. It was so fun to be able to relax while I was out with him.

I'd never been the one holding a secret, but somehow, perhaps it always felt like something was always hovering over us. That night, everything felt different, it felt just about perfect.

When we finished dinner we decided to go back to his place to take a moonlit walk in the gardens. As we held hands strolling through the floral paths I realized how much I loved him. He may have been a defective jerk, but he was my defective jerk.

The moonlight coupled with the colorful floodlights and the stars made for an enchanting trio. Everything felt magical, almost as if I were in a wonderland of bright lights and roses.

"Jerrica… Jerrica…have you heard a single word I've said in the past five minutes?" Jason tugged my hand firmly and I realized I'd been off in my own little world.

"I'm so sorry. This place, it's just so beautiful."

"So are you," he said as he stared at me with his beautiful steel blue eyes. I reached up to put my arms around his neck. He grabbed me firmly around the waist as he leaned down to kiss me with a demanding look on his face.

His warm mouth felt like velvet against mine. I pulled away from him briefly and we stared at each other silently before he kissed me again, this time filling my mouth with tongue, probing it passionately.

I was swept away in the intensity of him, and reached my hand around, grabbing his ass and pulling him closer to my pelvis. His fingers reached up to unbutton my blouse as his lips found their way from my lips down to my neck.

I untucked his shirt from his pants and reached my hands up underneath, tracing his muscular abs, gripping them as I made my way toward his chest. Once I couldn't reach any higher, I lifted his shirt up over his head and tossed it into the grass behind him.

Once Jason released the last button from its hole, he slowly slid my blouse back over my shoulders, letting it fall to the ground. I felt so vulnerable standing there in the moonlight as he stared at me silently while he unhooked my bra and exposed my heaving breasts.

My hardened nipples ached for him, and I moaned as he tugged on them and tweaked them with his fingertips. Passion overtook me, and I grabbed at his belt ferociously, trying to release him from the confines of his pants.

Hearing his zipper open was like music to my ears. I reached inside and felt his rock-hard cock for the first time in my hands. It was even bigger than I had ever imagined. So big that I worried that I might not be able to handle him, and I prayed he'd be gentle with me.

In an instant he grabbed his tie and wrapped it around my wrists, attaching me to a nearby tree. Both fear and excitement washed over me. I stared at him, desperate for him to touch me, but curious about what was coming next. He stared at me before he reached forward and pulled my skirt and panties to the ground.

I stood there with my hands above my head, watching him as he stared up at me. I thought he was about to stand up when his warm, wet tongue slid along my folds and wrapped itself around my clit. I moaned as I tried to lean down closer to his mouth while he lapped up my wetness and juices.

The tie restrained me so that I couldn't push against him as hard as I wanted to. I rocked my hips in excitement while my pussy tingled and ached to be filled by his throbbing cock. I could see it from where I stood, just sticking out waiting for me.

I kept staring at it while he licked away at me and sucked on my clit. I was thinking about what it would feel like to have him pumping in and out of me. When he shoved his stiff tongue into my soaking wet pussy I almost screamed out in ecstasy.

Desperation was creeping into my body and I needed to have him. I was aching so bad for him, and he knew it. He kept looking up at me, smiling as he licked and flicked away while my body jerked in reaction. He stood up and wrapped his hand around my neck.

"Do you want my cock, Jerrica?"

"Yes, Jason."

"Tell me, Jerrica," he said as its hardness pressed against my leg.

"I want your cock, Jason," I said. The excitement I felt from having his hand grasping at my throat while his cock rested just inches away from my hungry pussy was setting my body on fire.

"Beg me," he said as he stood close enough for his dick to tease my clit.

"Please fuck me," I begged.

"That's not convincing enough," he said as he stared at me with a disappointed expression on his face.

"Please fuck me now, Jason," I begged, with the desperation flowing from my lips.

He reached down and grabbed my legs, lifting them up and thrusting himself into me. As he thrust himself into me, my back pounded against the tree. I knew the roughness of the bark was leaving bruises, but I didn't care. All that mattered was being wrapped up in Jason's love.

His tongue sent shivers up and down my spine as it moved slowly along the crevices of my neck. I wanted to reach out to touch him with my hands, but my silken shackles prevented me from that one burning desire.

It felt so good finally giving myself to him, knowing that he was the one. I felt a fire burning within my core and I knew I was going to come soon as his kisses sizzled against my hot skin. His breathing was getting deeper as he pounded himself into me and thrust me harder against the tree.

I moaned and whimpered from both pleasure and pain as his hand slapped down hard on my ass cheek, causing it to jiggle slightly. I squealed out in delight from the raw pleasure it stirred up within me, while my body started taking over.

The heat rose with me and my breathing got shallower. My eyes were rolling back in my head as he thrust deeper and moaned louder. I started trying to rock my hips harder against him as the pleasure waves rolled throughout my body.

My hot, pulsating pussy engulfed his engorged and throbbing cock, making him groan louder as he pounded me against the tree. Finally, he let out a deep groan before pumping me full of load after load of his velvety cum. As it dripped out onto my thighs, I threw my head back and let out a gasp.

He untied me and we collapsed in the grass, surrounded by the scent of gardenias until we finally regained the strength to get dressed and return to the house.

Chapter 11 ~ Jason

AFTER JERRICA AND I made up everything was perfect. Our relationship became a whirlwind of romance like I'd never known. I'd never been happier in my life and I knew that I had met the perfect woman.

When it came closer to Liz's move-out date, I kept trying to talk her into moving in with me. But no matter how many times I tried to convince her, she kept saying no.

I kept asking her what was holding her back. I knew that something was keeping her from wanting to live with me, but I knew that she needed a roommate. Things were great between us, and I couldn't figure out why she wouldn't want us to be together all the time.

It became clear to me that she was old-fashioned, which is something I should've known earlier. The more I thought about it the more I realized she would never live with me unless we were engaged or married. I knew I had to come up with something spectacular in order to win her over. But I didn't know if I'd be able to think of something that would woo her.

One day when I was at work, the perfect idea came to me. I knew exactly what I had to do and I knew how to do it. I called Julie into my office.

"Oh, Jason, what do you need now?" Julie asked as she stared at me with a quizzical look on her face.

I told Julie my plan. "So," I asked, "do you think you can help me pull this off?"

"I think you're crazy," she said. "But this girl obviously loves you and your plan is so crazy it just might work. I'll see what I can do."

Chapter 12 ~ Jason

THE FOLLOWING FRIDAY THE office was in a frenzy preparing for the series launch of *The Educators*. In the afternoon a few hours before the first episode went live we had a live screening in the boardroom. As we were watching it, there was a loud noise outside and everyone turned toward the window.

"What is that?" Jerrica asked as she got up to look out the window.

"I'll worry about it later. Now we should finish the screening, make sure everything's okay before the big moment."

"But what is that thing?" she said again as she shook her head.

I turned up the volume on the TV to try to distract her. She kept looking back and forth between the window and the screen. Finally, I knew I was going to have to go out there in order to give her peace of mind. "I'll be right back," I said as I headed out of the room. I zoomed over to Julie's desk as she laughed with tears streaming down her face.

"How's it going in there?" she asked.

"All according to plan, Julie. All according to plan."

She reached into her top drawer and pulled out the ring. "Here, you go," she said as she patted me on the shoulder. "Should I tell the drone to leave now?"

"No, wait till I get back in there," I said. "Oh God, Julie, I'm so nervous. What if she says no?"

"Well then you just made a very public fool of yourself, Mr. Donnelly."

"Thanks for kicking me while I'm down, Julie," I said as I shrugged my shoulders.

"Don't worry so much. Any girl would be lucky to have you," she said. "Now, you go in there and get her."

I threw my shoulders back, took a deep breath, and walked back to the boardroom. When I walked in Jerrica was wide-eyed, wanting to know what was outside. "Just a drone with the delivery," I said. "No big deal."

"A drone," she said, nodding.

"Yeah, it's really nothing. Let's get back to the screening."

"What?" she asked.

"Just something we needed for a prop for the episode," I said. "It's not important.

I pressed play so we could finish the screening.

"Wait a minute," Jerrica said. "I don't remember this scene. Why are they all just sitting on a bench?"

"All this was an add-in scene at the last minute," I said.

"Everything goes past my desk. I don't understand why this wasn't run by me first."

"Sometimes I have to take the lead. It's called Donnelly Multimedia for a reason."

"Seriously, Jason, that's just not fair. I worked so hard on that series and just…"

"Just shut up and keep watching, Jerrica. Please."

She folded her arms in front of herself and I could see her face turning redder as she got angrier and angrier.

All the characters were sitting on a bench waiting for a bus when they suddenly held up newspapers. Written across the front of the newspapers was "WILL YOU MARRY ME" written in big letters.

I knelt down beside her and pulled the ring out of my pocket as I paused the screen.

"Well," I asked, "will you?"

Everyone in the boardroom sat and stared at us, waiting for her answer…

The end of Billionaire Seeks An Heir Book 2: Unraveled Lives

Read Book 3 – Unforgettable Melody

Thanks for Reading!

Thank you for purchasing my book. It's that sort of support that allows me to continue doing something that I love every day. If you liked the read, please consider leaving a review so more people can find and enjoy it too!

Want More of Misha's books? Join Misha's Newsletter and you'll always be notified about new releases ~

www.mishacarver.com/newsletter

About the Author

I love to write stories about powerful men and women and the romances fiascos they find themselves in. Whether it's billionaires, shifters, bad boys, or just ordinary people, they'll make their way into one of my books.

So many stories flood my imagination every day. I love to write them down so other people can enjoy them too. For me writing isn't a job. When I write, I see the stories playing out in my head. It's almost like going to the movies for free. I hope you have the same experience when you read them.

Also By Misha Carver

Shifter/Paranormal Romances
Purrfect Mates Series
Purrfect Chaos (Book 1)

Purrfect Storm (Book 2)

Purrfect Harmony (Book 3)

Purrfect Mates Box Set

Contemporary/New Adult Romances
Billionaire Seeks An Heir Series
Unplanned Fairy Tale (Book 1)

Unraveled Lives (Book 2)

Unforgettable Melody (Book 3)

Billionaire Seeks An Heir Boxed Set Collection

Big City Heat Firefighter Series

Light My Fire (Book 1)

I'm On Fire (Book 2)

Ring of Fire (Book 3)

Standalone Romance Novellas

Sasha's Storm – (steamy romance)

Holiday Romances

Second Chance Christmas Romances

The Christmas Homecoming (Book 1)

The Christmas Reunion (Book 2)

The Christmas Spirit (Book 3)

Jingle Bell Shifters

Jingle Bell Growl (Book 1)

Jingle Bell Howl (Book 2)

Jingle Bell Prowl (Book 3)

www.ingramcontent.com/pod-product-compliance
Lightning Source LLC
Chambersburg PA
CBHW022107050726
47591CB00002B/709